For my grandmother,
with honey and cinnamon

Published by
Princeton Architectural Press
A McEvoy Group company
202 Warren Street
Hudson, New York 12534
Visit our website at www.papress.com

First published in Canada under the title *Le chemin de la montagne*
Text and illustrations © 2017 Marianne Dubuc
Translation rights arranged through VeroK Agency, Barcelona, Spain

English edition © 2018 Princeton Architectural Press
All rights reserved
Printed and bound in China
21 20 19 18 4 3 2 1 First edition

ISBN 978-1-61689-723-9

Princeton Architectural Press is a leading publisher in architecture,
design, photography, landscape, and visual culture. We create fine
books and stationery of unsurpassed quality and production values.
With more than one thousand titles published, we find design
everywhere and in the most unlikely places.

This book was illustrated using pencil, colored pencil,
and watercolor.

Editor: Nina Pick
Typesetting: Paul Wagner

Special thanks to: Ryan Alcazar, Janet Behning, Nolan Boomer,
Abby Bussel, Benjamin English, Jan Cigliano Hartman, Susan Hershberg,
Kristen Hewitt, Lia Hunt, Valerie Kamen, Jennifer Lippert, Sara McKay,
Eliana Miller, Wes Seeley, Sara Stemen, Marisa Tesoro, and
Joseph Weston of Princeton Architectural Press
—Kevin C. Lippert, publisher

Library of Congress Cataloging-in-Publication Data
available upon request.

Up the Mountain Path

marianne dubuc

PRINCETON ARCHITECTURAL PRESS

NEW YORK

Mrs. Badger is very old.
She's seen many things.
Some can be found in her kitchen.

pottery shard

smooth pebble

sand from the sea

finch nest

Her house is at the foot of a small mountain.

Every Sunday she walks the path from her garden
to the mountain's peak.

Mountain Path

Bridge Lane

Sweetwater Stream

Linden Tree Promenade

It's a Sunday like any other.
Maybe a little sunnier.

"The mountain again,
Mrs. Badger?"

"Hello, Frederic."

Frederic is a white-throated sparrow.
He lives in Mrs. Badger's garden.

On her way Mrs. Badger picks mushrooms
for her friend Alexander.

She will bring them to him later. He will be delighted.

"Oh, thank you!"

Mrs. Badger knows all about mushrooms.

Boletus

delicious in
ragout

Amanita muscaria

CAUTION!
Poison!

Sometimes Mrs. Badger
finds a friend in need.

She helps the best she can...

and continues
on her way.

Every Sunday is the same.

But today she has a feeling she
is being watched.

"There's enough
for both of us, if
you're hungry."

Mrs. Badger shares everything,
even her snack.

"Is it true that you have climbed to the top of the mountain?"

"Yes, it's called Sugarloaf Peak."

"I'd like to go up there too."

"You'll see. It's wonderful."

"You look worried,
little one."

Mrs. Badger can tell when something is wrong.

"I'm too
small."

For Mrs. Badger,
nothing is impossible.

"I was your age when
I climbed the mountain
for the first time."

But sometimes it's hard
to have faith.

And so Mrs. Badger continues
on her own.

And hop!

"I'd really like to see what's up there."

Mrs. Badger understands.

"With the right stick it's easier."

"What's your name?"

"Lulu."

THE PERFECT STICK

made of hardwood,
for strength

soft bark for
the paws

an extra
little twig

perfect length

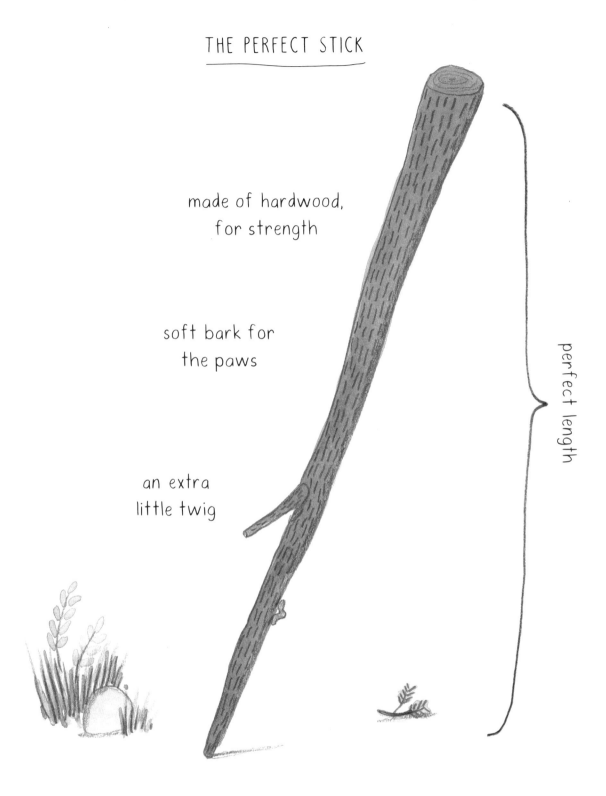

On this sunlit Sunday, Mrs. Badger has a companion on the trail.

"Careful, it's slippery!"

"Why do trees have leaves?"

"To greet the sun."

"Where are the ants going?"

"Where the road leads them."

Lulu asks a lot of questions.

"Look what I found. Can I eat it?"

"That's Suzie!"

Mrs. Badger teaches Lulu
to listen instead.

Tu-Ti-Tu turlututurlutu!

"That's Frederic!"

"It's pretty!"

"Mamaaaa!!!"

Mrs. Badger also teaches Lulu how to help.

"Thank you!"

"Here's your little one, Mrs. Bird."

"Mama!"

Lulu is a quick learner.

On the way, choices have to be made.

"Which path do we take?"

"Which one do you like best?"

Mrs. Badger knows that life is made up of decisions.

"I'd like to go this way. It smells like apples."

And that you have to listen to your heart.

"What will we see
up there?"

The world!

"It must be incredible to be at
the top of the world!"

"Oh, it makes you feel
really small."

"Small as a hummingbird?"

"Smaller."

"Small as an ant?"

"Smaller."

"Small as what?"

"Small as a speck of stardust shimmering on the morning dew."

Mrs. Badger is also a poet.

"The ants go marching one by one,
hurrah, hurrah…"

Mrs. Badger knows how to raise
the morale of the troops.

"Are you all right,
little one?"

Sometimes songs are not enough.

"I have somewhere
to show you."

The troops, especially those with
small feet, are exhausted.

So Lulu and Mrs. Badger stop for a little while to catch their breath.

After a short rest, their energy returns.

"Shall we continue?"

"It isn't much farther."

It is a sunny Sunday, and soon they
will reach the top.

"Almost there,
Mrs. Badger!"

"Hello, Will!"

Will is a turkey vulture.
He lives on Sugarloaf Peak
and has known Mrs. Badger
for a long time.

little, bare,
red head

piercing
but kindly
eyes

sharp claws

The final stretch is the most difficult.

"It's very high!"

"You can do it,
Lulu!"

Lulu doesn't say a word.
She's on top of the world.

From then on, every Sunday they climb
to Sugarloaf Peak together.

"Sugarloaf again, Lulu?"

"Good morning, Frederic!"

"Nice to meet you,
Mrs. Turtle!"

Mrs. Badger shares with Lulu all
the secrets of the mountain.

"This is sumac."

"Can we make
lemonade with it?"

These past few weeks it's been Mrs. Badger's
turn to need a rest.

"Are you okay?"

Lulu takes a moment to stop for her.

But whatever happens, they always reach
the top of the mountain.

"Do you think Will is
going to be there?"

"He said
he would be."

"Careful!
It's slippery."

"We're almost there!"

"It's wonderful!"

Then, one sunny Sunday, Mrs. Badger doesn't
have the strength to climb to Sugarloaf Peak.

"Go by yourself. When you return,
you can tell me everything."

So Lulu follows the
mountain path…

the same as every Sunday.
But not quite.

Week after week, Lulu explores the mountain...

and its secrets.

When she returns she tells Mrs. Badger
all about her discoveries.

She also brings new treasures.

Gradually Mrs. Badger's mountain becomes
Lulu's mountain.

One day, at a fork in the road, Lulu discovers
a path she had never noticed.

"It smells like
raspberries!"

"There's enough for
two, you know."

"I have a wonderful place
to show you."